Brunswick, Maryland: Ghosts, Myths, and Legends of a Historic Railroad Town

James R. Castle

Maryland Memories, LLC

October 2020

Brunswick, Maryland:
Ghosts, Myths, and Legends of a Historic Railroad Town

James R. Castle

James R. Castle
PO Box 8
Brunswick, MD 21716

www.Jamesrcastle.com
www.facebook.com/authorjamesrcastle
Email: jamesrcastle@comcast.net

DEDICATION

To you, unknown spirits, who wish so badly to communicate with me. I wish so badly to communicate with you.

Someday, we will talk.

Table of Contents

PRELUDE

AND SO, IT BEGINS......

The geological formation sets the foundation, while the Potomac River provides the conduit for energy to spread over land that was once home to native people. Settlers homesteaded here and the Chesapeake and Ohio Canal channeled even more energy into this village. The Civil War stained our timeline and the Baltimore and Ohio Railroad created a most dangerous working environment. Many began to call Brunswick their home, and some, partook in murder and mayhem. But most participated in the social graces of the Victorian and Edwardian eras. All of these aspects, combined, make Brunswick, Maryland the perfect haunted location.

The stage is set, and the curtain opens. Enjoy!

CHAPTER 1

A BRIEF HISTORY OF BRUNSWICK

The native people knew the great benefits of this area. The Potomac River provided various species of fish, especially eels, for food. The river flats provided hunting locations, drinkable water from streams, and gathering plants for food and healing. Native plants still grow here, and the natural hills created a safe place to watch over the territory. A territory worth fighting other tribes for control.

Very little is known about the natives who called this area home. We do know that they were Susquehannock, an Iroquois speaking group of Native Americans. In this area, they were here as late as the 1720s and bartered with European traders such as Abraham Pennington, who called this area his home temporarily in the 1720s.

The Natives called this place "Eel Pot" and "Buffalo Wallows". "Eel Pot", referred to the numerous eel traps the natives successfully used in the area and "Buffalo Wallows" was the area buffalo stood in the Potomac River near what is now the Brunswick Family Campground.

Numerous land grants made up what is now the greater Brunswick area. They included "Merryland", "Coxson's Rest", and "Hawkins' Merry Peep O Day". The area was well known for ferry service across the Potomac River, earning the location early names such as "German Crossing" and "Potomac Crossing". The area and ferry changed hands many times until it was transferred to Leonard Smith in 1780. Smith was familiar with this area as he earlier platted "New Town", later called "Traptown", now called Jefferson. In 1787, Smith platted 96 lots for a town he named Berlin. Berlin, along the Potomac, was marketed much like a resort, encouraging folks to get away from the swamp of Washington, DC to enjoy life along the river. Slowly, the town increased in population and had several businesses, including a prosperous flour mill.

Berlin was a hamlet, in that Smith never reserved a building lot for a church or built a church as part of his small planned community.[1] These early homesteaders lived off the land and river, much like the natives did before them. The potential of greater commerce was a "fire" fueled by the speculation that the B&O Railroad and C&O Canal were to pass through Berlin. This premise bore true as the B&O acquired the lots needed for track right of way through the middle of the village. Foreshadowing a race to the finish line, the C&O Canal Company purchased lots for the future canal location.

Ironically, the B&O Railroad Company and the C&O Canal Company broke ground on the same day; July 4, 1828. Both forms of transportation arrive in Berlin around 1834, where both companies had engaged in a fierce legal battle for the use of such a narrow strip of land along the Potomac River from Point of Rocks, MD to Harpers Ferry, VA. A legal compromise allowed both companies to use the right of way. The B&O Railroad constructed a small warehouse in Berlin and only employed a small section gang locally. A section gang is a group of workers responsible for maintenance along a specific section of track.

---

[1]Funk, H.B., Smith: Way Before We Were Brunswick

Berlin was primarily a canal town with the canal greatly assisting an agriculture economy, supported by a mill producing high quality flour for transportation along the canal's approximate 184.5 miles. The population was about 300 at the time of the Civil War.

Slavery was prevalent here with the Petersville District (in which Berlin was a part) registering 78 slaves in the 1860 census. The area was comprised of large lots that needed tending, and slaves did most of that work. The main crop grown here was wheat, which made high quality flour and that flour was processed at Wenner's mill along the river and canal. There was much activity here during the Civil War, and that information is presented in a later chapter.

The photo on the previous page is from the late 1890's and shows the B&O Railroad tracks, the C&O Canal, the Potomac River, and the Brunswick Bridge. Photo from the Brunswick Heritage Museum.

The B&O Railroad's Big Decision

In the late 1880s, B&O Railroad officials began appearing in Berlin, and the community knew something was afoot. Land speculators offered to purchase land in flood-prone areas of the village. These buyers, working for the railroad, had soon successfully purchased much of the land surrounding Berlin and lots within the village. Shortly after that, the B&O Railroad announced that Berlin would be the location for its new main classification yard. Recognizing that confusion existed having two Berlins in Maryland, the other Berlin located on the eastern shore, our Berlin was changed to Brunswick.

Who determined the name of Brunswick is speculation. There is a Brunswick Germany (Braunschweig). The prevailing hypothesis is that railroad management wanted to keep the name tied to the German heritage of the name Berlin.

The relocation of the main classification yard meant that many workers would be needed for the expansion. With that need, a "Boom Town" emerged. There was a need for housing, stores, churches, organizations, etc. to be quickly constructed. Over time, most of the area of Berlin was acquired (and in some cases taken), dismantled, and rebuilt on Brunswick's higher altitude streets. The success of the B&O Railroad in Brunswick closely mirrored the success of the nation. For example, the railroad industry would boom during World War I and World War II. It felt the severe decline during the Great Depression, and layoffs and furloughs were prevalent during times of decline in the railroad industry. While many Brunswick residents thought the 1950s was a bustling age for the town, the railroad industry was actually on the decline. The annual payroll, in 1959, for Brunswick railroaders was approximately $6 million. Within a decade that payroll was drastically reduced as the decision to move the yard operation out of Brunswick was instituted.

The only railroading aspect that saved Brunswick from turning into a ghost town was passenger service along the Metropolitan Branch to Washington, DC. In the 1970s railroad workers moved their families out of Brunswick for the sake of finding work. They ended up leaving behind enormous Victorian homes. These homes were purchased by folks who could work along the Metropolitan Branch in such places as Germantown, Gaithersburg, Rockville, Silver Spring, and Washington, D.C. This situation created folks' opportunity to earn "city money" but live in a more rural area.

This photo, circa 1900, shows the Victorian home, located on 9th Avenue, of the Stewart Family. Photo from the Brunswick History Commission

Since the departure of the railroad as a major employer, Brunswick has struggled with its identity. What seems as a simple task of being a place that embraces its past and welcomes the future, it has been a concept that has failed to materialize.

One thing is for sure. The "voices" of Brunswick's past will never be silenced, as long as there are those who wish to communicate with the spirits that those voices belong.

"Black Schoolhouse in Brunswick, MD". Photo from the Brunswick History Commission

Now knowing a basic history of Brunswick, the time has arrived to delve into Brunswick's paranormal realm.

CHAPTER 2

HAUNTED HERITAGE

This 1904 photo shows the newly constructed Red Men's Hall in Brunswick. Note the small shacks to the left of the building. Photo from the Brunswick Heritage Museum.

At 2:00 am one morning, the phone rings.

"Hey Jim!", says the caller. "Yeah man?", I answer. "I need to go down to the museum and turn the lights out because someone left them on.", the caller stated. "Sure, but why you calling me?", I asked. The answer was, "Man, I ain't going in the building at night by myself!"

The caller had good reason to be nervous because the old Brunswick Red Men's Hall, now known as the Brunswick Heritage Museum, is haunted. There is plenty of evidence to support that statement.

Red Men's Hall

Constructed in 1904, the Red Men's Hall was the centerpiece of Brunswick's social culture. Before 1890, Brunswick was called Berlin, and within old Berlin, along the railroad track, was the Opera House. The Opera House was the location where Berliners came to enjoy entertainment such as plays, music, lectures, and banquets. At some point, the crowds' weight became too heavy, and the floors began to buckle, causing the building to be condemned. The building was later destroyed by fire. The townsfolk of Brunswick demanded a replacement building to be used as the social center of the town. During this same time, the Improved Order of Red Men, Delaware Tribe #43, Berlin, MD, organized in 1867, was housed in a little wooden shack by the railroad track, now South Virginia Avenue. When the railroad expanded the yard in the early 1900s, the Red Men's building's front door opened up upon the new tracks. A new home for the Red Men was needed.

This photo shows the original Red Men's Hall in Berlin. The building still exists today at the foot of South Maryland Ave. Photo from The Brunswick Heritage Museum.

From 1904 until prohibition, Red Men's Hall was the center of all social activity in Brunswick. When the new building opened, it was the most impressive building constructed in Brunswick. A life-sized Cigar Store Indian was perched above

the door and the large letters "IORM" (Improved Order of Red Men) above the windows. Two businesses were housed on the street level as well as one in the lower level. The second floor was an open floor plan that allowed for large crowds to gather. The third floor also had an open floor plan but contained a stage area for presentations. This floor was mainly used for the Red Men. Most activities held at the old Opera House were now held at the Hall in addition to school functions, including graduations.

In 1936, the Red Men sold the building to the

Fraternal Order of the Eagles. This time, the second floor operated as their bar and the third floor as their social hall. In 1969, the Eagles moved to SCOB (Social Club of Brunswick) Park, where they are currently located today.

The photo on the opposite page shows the Eagles Club bar located on the second floor of Red Men's Hall. While the bar is no longer located there, the architectural elements remain. Photo from the Brunswick. Heritage Museum.

The Brunswick Potomac Foundation was incorporated in 1969. The foundation organized the Potomac River Heritage Festivals, which has now morphed into the annual Brunswick Railroad Days. One of the popular aspects of the festival was that local townsfolk would provide historical artifacts related to the town's history and place them on display in the local businesses' front windows. From this practice, the idea of a local museum was born. In 1974, the Brunswick Potomac Foundation purchased the Red Men's Hall from the Brunswick Eagles to establish a town museum. The Museum, which is now known as the Brunswick Heritage Museum is comprised of a Museum Store, and the C&O Canal and Brunswick Visitor Centers. The visitor centers are located on the street level. The basement level contains a business and storage for the Museum. The second floor displays historical artifacts relating to the history of Berlin and Brunswick. The third floor is home to the Museum's highlight, a large HO scale model train layout, depicting the B&O Railroad's Metropolitan Branch from Union Station in Washington D.C. to Harpers Ferry in West Virginia, circa 1959.

It was in the 1970s that we first know of a documented report of paranormal activity at the Museum. A young lady visited the Museum with her family, and she sat in an old wooden chair in the Museum Store. When she looked at the doorway, leading to the stairs, she saw a lady in Victorian clothing walk past the doorway, glancing at her while she passed. The girl thought it was a volunteer dressed in Victorian period clothing. However, when she said something about it to the store volunteer, she was informed that there were no other female volunteers in the Museum at that time. It was the first reported sighting of the infamous "Lady in White" at the Brunswick Museum. The "Lady in White" has made her appearance known for over 45 years with numerous reports of her sightings from volunteers, staff, and museum visitors. Just who is the "Lady in White" and why is she at the Museum? We may be close to finding out the answers to these questions.

Before 2015, very few paranormal investigators were allowed access to the museum. In that year the Museum Board of Directors began to allow paranormal investigators access to the building.

The rules are simple; the President of the Museum, who is also a paranormal investigator, must be present; there is no conjuring or provoking of spirits. There are no seances or Ouija boards used; there are no open flames ever used; and no artifacts are to be handled by anyone other than Museum volunteers. The Museum has been host to numerous paranormal teams local to Maryland and as far away as North Carolina. Some of these teams have included Elite Paranormal from Keedysville, MD; The Maryland Society for Paranormal Research from Brunswick, MD; and The Association of Paranormal Study from Raleigh, NC. One notable team to investigate the Museum is The Ghost Pit from Franklin County, Pennsylvania.

Brian Philips and Sue Byers created the Ghost Pit. Team members include those with psychic abilities, investigators, and a historian. The team first investigated the Museum in 2017. After an investigation, Brian and Sue inquired if the Museum was open to the concept of a monthly investigation, open to the public for a fee, where the public would learn how to use equipment while investigating the Museum building. The Board of Directors gave enthusiastic approval. The paranormal evidence collected by the Ghost Pit and other investigators at the building has been outstanding.

One hotspot in the building is the basement. More specifically, an old bathroom in the basement seems to be the home of the "Tall Man". Numerous psychics have described a very tall man being present in the basement. The Ghost Pit has mapped the figure, using an SLS camera. An SLS camera is a structured light camera that uses distance detection and thermal temperature sensing to map out human shapes that cannot be seen with the naked eye.

There is also the "Grumpy Man" in the basement. This unhappy fellow makes himself known to many visitors through spirit box sessions, sometimes belting out expletives, stating that he "wants to be left the F**K alone." Objects in the basement have been moved across the floor as if they were kicked. This activity is attributed to the "Grumpy Man".

An extraordinary moment happened while conducting a flashlight session in the basement with Robert Murphy of Elite Paranormal. While this author is not a fan of flashlight sessions, often describing the technique as a "Victorian parlor trick", the method can be successful when used scientifically as Robert does. On one particular night, Robert and I loosened the caps on three flashlights that were color-coded red, green, and yellow. After asking a series of questions, the green light lit when asked if the spirit present was female. Robert thanked the woman and requested she please turn the light off, which she did. Robert then asked if the spirit was male and received no response.

He then asked if the spirit was female to please turn on the red flashlight. The red flashlight illuminated. He thanked her and requested that she turn off the light, which she did.

He then asked if the spirit was male to turn on the red flashlight. No lights turned on. Robert then asked if the spirit was female to please turn on the yellow flashlight. The light on the yellow flashlight turned on. Again, very politely, Robert asked if she would turn off the light, which she did.

The reason for the multiple, alternating questions is to create a more scientific test to rule out random occurrences of the lights illuminating. This particular interaction was not random, we were communicating with a female spirit.

I verbally asked if the spirit was of a particular person, naming at least twenty five female names associated with the museum, and there was no answer from our spirit. Robert then asked if our female friend was still with us, and the red flashlight illuminated. He thanked her and asked that she turn the light off, which she did. Thinking I had exhausted my list of possible suspects for this female spirit, my memory recollected one of our founders' name. I mentioned the name, and immediately the green flashlight turned on. During the positive reaction of guessing the name, the flashlight turned off. Robert then asked numerous questions as to why the spirit remained at the Museum. "Are you mad we don't serve food down here anymore?" "Are you mad at the condition of the basement?" "Are you looking for someone particular?" We both asked numerous questions. As we were about to give up, I remembered that this person would have interacted with the Museum's former President, the late Lee B. Smith. "Are you upset that Lee Smith is no longer the Museum President?", I asked. The red light brightly illuminated. Robert thanked her for her answer and requested that she extinguish the light and she did so.

Satisfied with our session, we started to end when Robert posed a final question. "You do know James is doing the best he can to run the museum, right?" The black flashlight turned on faintly. Robert asked if she could make the light brighter, which she did. One last time he thanked her and requested that she turn off the light. She again obliged. Robert and I said goodnight and goodbye and ended this very memorable session.

Numerous psychics have picked up upon a woman they describe as dressed from the 1970s and seems concerned about the Museum artifacts. This spirit is undoubtedly the spirit of the same Museum founder that Robert and I communicated within the basement.

When investigating the Museum, all of the

teams use the main floor as their "home base" or "hub". This location is where they place their personal items, store equipment, set up tv monitors, etc. Since the front door and bathrooms are located on this floor, it is also where the teams take breaks and gather to discuss the progress of investigations. This floor does not get investigated as much as the other floors, but it is no less haunted than other building parts. Each time an investigator "hunts" on the main floor, they are successful in capturing evidence. One such time was when an amateur investigator recorded an EVP (electronic voice phenomena) of an adolescent boy saying, "If it's in the cupboard, then it's in the cupboard".

Also, on the main floor is where a group of amateur investigators was participating in a Ghost Pit monthly investigation, when over the spirit box came the words "Get out". Brian instructed everyone to take steps backward to comply with the request. One young man took a step forward and felt a burning sensation on his chest. When exposed, it was discovered he had been scratched on his chest. Brian explained to the group that spirits are no different from living beings in which if one backs someone into a corner, their instinct is to fight. This same principle applies to spirits in that they are not demonstrating evil or demonic activity. Instead, the spirit requested the group to leave or get out. When the spirit felt threatened, it defended itself by scratching the young man.

This photo shows an SLS camera mapping out a figure on a barber chair on the Museum's second floor. Is a Brunswick railroader trying to get a haircut at the old YMCA? Photo from The Ghost Pit.

The second floor of the Museum is the most active in the building. This fact makes sense as the room had been the center of social activity in Brunswick for over 100 years. The library of EVP's (electronic voice phenomena) from the second floor fills numerous thumb drives. Children playing, railroaders waiting on trains, glasses clanking, muffled conversations, thrown F-bombs, "Brunswick", "Berlin", have all been recorded over the years on the second floor. Numerous figures have been mapped out on SLS cameras. The second floor has also provided us some very memorable moments.

Another photo from The Ghost Pit showing a figure mapped while sitting in a chair in an exhibit of a railroad office. Is this railroader still working at his desk?

When the Association of Paranormal Study visited the Museum from Raleigh, North Carolina, Alex Matsuo and her team positioned themselves near an exhibit interpreting Victorian period mourning rituals. The display exhibited many local artifacts including textiles, mourning jewelry, photographs of deceased loved ones, and a child's coffin from the local mortuary. The coffin was a wooden box where infants were placed for viewing. However, the bodies were buried in another box or casket. This particular coffin may have displayed a hundred children at the local funeral home. These artifacts retain energy and attachments that wanted to communicate with Alex. As the RF (radio field) meters spiked on the coffin, Alex recorded a woman's sigh. On a later investigation and after the child's coffin was placed into storage, Elite Paranormal was attracted to a storage area where they felt a spirit was located. That storage area contained the child's casket. On a later investigation, Brian of the Ghost Pit mapped a figure on his SLS camera in the coffin's storage area. There is, without a doubt, spirits attached to the child's coffin at the Brunswick Heritage Museum.

The second floor is also home to the "Woman in White". One of the most talented mediums I know, Sharon Renner Lewis of Guidance and Insight with Sharon, participated in a Ghost Pit investigation when she sensed a woman on the second floor, dressed in a white blouse and a black Victorian skirt. Our mysterious "Woman in White"! This woman roams the museum, not understanding the "Museum" concept of the building. She paces near the windows because she is looking for something. Another medium stated that our "Woman in White" stares out the window because "she can see his grave from there".

The goal for the first year of public investigations at the Museum was to document whether the building is haunted. That answer is yes. The second year of investigating was dedicated to finding out just who or what is haunting the museum. We have accomplished that goal. The next step in will be to identify why these folks are spending their eternity at the Brunswick Heritage Museum in downtown Brunswick.

This photo shows Red Men's Hall near the completion of construction in 1904. The building is now the Brunswick Heritage Museum. Photo from the Brunswick Heritage Museum.

CHAPTER 3

WALTER'S SPIRIT

It was the end of a busy Saturday night at Smoketown Brewing Station. Numerous workers were finishing their cleaning and closing duties when a crash was heard from the kitchen. Several staff members ran to the kitchen to find no one there, but they did find a stack of trays had fallen on the floor. The trays were stacked correctly upon a flat table and should not have fallen for any reason. Both employees shared a look, both knowing who knocked the pizza trays on the floor...it was Walter again.

The Old Brunswick Fire Hall

Smoketown Brewing Station is located in what the locals refer to as "The Old Brunswick Fire Hall". Brunswick's first fire hall was built on what is now North Delaware Avenue. It is in a building that was at one time owned by the Knights of the Pythias, an early Brunswick fraternal organization. In the 1940s, members of the Brunswick Volunteer

Fire Company knew they needed a new building. Constructing the new fire hall was a labor of love and dedication to public service as the Frederick County government refused to provide funding for the new building. At that time, the Fire Chief, Sonny Cannon, a very strong personality, wasn't going to let the lack of funding stop the needed progress of the Brunswick Volunteer Fire Company. The fire company raised funds, gathered materials, and built the new fire hall regardless of the faced funding challenges. The new fire hall construction was completed in 1948.

This photo is from the Brunswick Heritage Museum. It shows Sonny Cannon's sound truck advertising the democratic ticket during the 1940s.

Sonny Cannon owned a sound truck. This truck traveled all over the tri-state area. Cannon could deliver an amplified advertising pitch or political message for people to hear. The truck would also be used for the connection of microphones so people and musicians could be heard. This line of work put Sonny Cannon in contact with those in the music industry, and those contacts were used to benefit the Brunswick Volunteer Fire Company. The primary fund raising mechanism for the Brunswick Fire Company in the 1950s and 1960s was dancing featuring live entertainment. Entertainers performed for an hour or so, and then tables near the front stage were moved to create a dance floor. Stars such as Guy Lombardo, Jimmy Dean, Roy Clark, and Little Jimmie Dickens graced the stage. The most famous celebrity to sing at the Brunswick Fire Hall was Patsy Cline.

The photo on the previous page is from the Smoketown History   Facebook page. It shows Patsy Cline, Brunswick Council Woman Nellie Roby, and Jimmy Dean backstage at the Old Brunswick Fire Hall.

Patsy Cline

As an up and coming singer, Virginia Hensley had an exclusive contract to perform at local Moose Clubs with musician Bill Peer and his Melody Boys in the early 1950s. It was Bill Peer who suggested Virginia change her first name to Patsy. Her last name was changed to Cline when she married Gerald Cline, whom she met at the Brunswick Moose Lodge. After landing a professional recording contract, Patsy Cline headlined a show along with Jimmy Dean at the Brunswick Fire Company for a fundraiser to pay for the medical treatment of a local child injured in a house fire. The very stage she sang upon is still on the second floor of the Old Brunswick Fire Hall, soon to be a social hall called "Sonny's", in honor of legendary Fire Chief Sonny Cannon.

After the City of Brunswick annexed Brunswick Crossing in the early 2000s, members of the Brunswick Volunteer Fire Company again, knew it needed a bigger station. The new Brunswick Fire Hall was constructed within the Brunswick Crossing housing development. The Old Brunswick Fire Hall was placed on the open real estate market for sale. After some time on the market, a purchaser came forward but a use for the building was not entirely known. After bouncing some ideas around with some buddies while drinking beer, a craft brewery dream was born.

David Blackmon, his family, and a work crew labored diligently to turn the Old Brunswick Fire Hall's first floor into a brewery. In April of 2016, a grand opening was held, and Smoketown Brewing Station officially opened its doors. Smoketown is a nickname bestowed upon Brunswick as the smoke from the locomotive steam engines, homes, and businesses covered the town in smoke during its railroading heyday.

A Spirit Appears

A few years later, Blackmon shared a story. One night as a workgroup was renovating the property, he looked up and saw an older, skinny man standing in the front engine bay area. Dave Blackmon told the gentleman that the brewery was not yet open, and the man seemed to disappear. Later, as various folks brought fire company memorabilia to be displayed at the brewery, a photo of Walter Rice was presented. Blackmon knew he saw the man before. The man in the photo was the older, skinny man he saw that night in the brewery. However, the story was not surprising to many current and former Brunswick Volunteer Fire Fighters who worked out of the Old Brunswick Fire Hall.

Walter Rice was a member of the Brunswick Volunteer Fire Company. He was a very reliable man and would serve as the Brunswick Fire Hall building's caretaker for Sonny Cannon. According to members of the Brunswick Volunteer Fire Company, Walter Rice did not approve of events in the fire hall that partook in alcohol drinking. He would often clean up after these events and watch over the building during them. When Fire Company members would run emergency calls, Walter would straighten up after the young men and clean the engine bay. During Brunswick's raucous 1950s and 1960s, there was no better way to ensure a reliable driver than to pay to have one on duty. During this time, Walter was a paid driver for the Brunswick Fire Company. His bunk room was off to the left of the engine bay, a room that still exists today. It was in this same bunk room where Walter passed away in his sleep. But it is strongly believed that his spirit has never left the Old Brunswick Fire Hall.

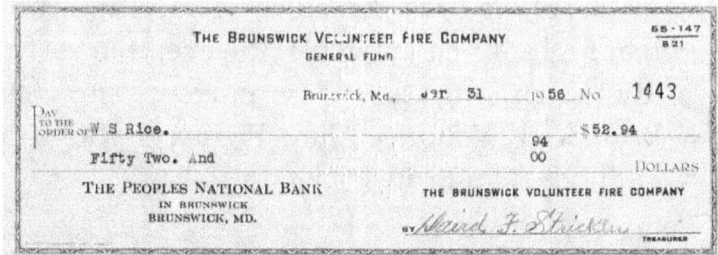

This is a paycheck to Walter Rice from 1956 for being a paid driver and caretaker for the Brunswick Volunteer Fire Company.

The photo on the previous page shows Walter Rice on the left and Sonny Cannon on the right posing with a group of young men. Walter wore his official hat often. Photo from Smoketown History Facebook Page.

If you speak to the Brunswick Fire Company members that operated out of the Old Fire Hall, most have Walter Rice stories. A paranormal investigator named Peter Gabriel convened a gathering of current and former members of the Brunswick Volunteer Fire Company together at Smoketown Brewing Station to discuss their Walter experiences. This author was lucky to be in the audience. Gabriel was the first paranormal investigator to investigate the Old Brunswick Fire Hall. Every creak and knock in the old building was attributed to Walter, but some events were undeniably unique.

For example, take the story of men sleeping in their bunks to awaken to a ghostly figure, shaped like Walter Rice, standing over them. Other firemen claim that they left the engine bay messy when they rolled out for a fire call and returned to a clean area, which would have been Walter's task as the caretaker. At the end of the presentation, members of the Maryland Society for Paranormal

Research arrived to investigate the building. After addressing the crowd on their investigative methods, this author and Peter Gabriel were invited to investigate. This author jumped at the chance to be part of the first team to investigate the building.

The First to Investigate

The tasting room was still active when the investigation began, so the group started on the second floor. At this time, construction had not yet started, and the second floor was wide open with a few brewing supplies stored there. The very first noticeable thing was that even the lowest volume of noise created by anyone located in the room was carried far in the open hall. Also noted was that sound from the tasting room carried upstairs, so capturing EVP's was not an option while the brewery was open.

As guests, Peter and I hung back amongst ourselves and watched members of the Maryland Society of Paranormal Research conduct their investigation. One particular technique used that night stoked my curiosity; dowsing rods.

In Robert Murphy's book, *Investigating the Paranormal Ghosts and Sprits*, he writes, "…people are learning that the rods are easily manipulated by the paranormal and can be another way to show contact." Most dowsing rods are made up of an L shaped piece of copper. Beads surround the handle to allow the users to hold the rods in an effort not to manipulate their direction. Murphy continues, "A common reaction to paranormal influence is for the rods to rotate slowly or quickly completely around."

The dowsing rod session was in full "swing" on the second floor of the Old Brunswick Fire Hall when I requested to ask some questions while another investigator held the rods. The team was kind enough to approve my request. At the beginning of the session, it is explained to the spirits that "crossing" the rods is a "yes" answer. The rods were perfectly still when I asked if anyone was here from the Brunswick Fire Company, but they slowly began to turn as soon as I had finished presenting the question. I quickly followed up with, "Does anyone know Sonny Cannon?" The rods crossed quickly. I asked for the spirit to uncross the dowsing rods, and the rods then straightened. "Are we speaking to Sonny Cannon?", I asked. The rods didn't budge a bit. "Are we speaking to Walter Rice?", I asked. Still, no movement with the rods. "Do you know of Walter Rice?", I quickly followed up. The rods began to cross slowly. "Were you a member of the Fire Company?", I eagerly queried. The rods then turned fast, spinning around in complete circles.

Many people volunteered at the Old Brunswick Fire Hall, and it seems like some still report for duty, including Walter Rice. Will you see or hear any of them there? Next time you visit Downtown Brunswick, stop into Smoketown Brewing Station. They have many brews that pay homage to Brunswick's history. Beers such as Berlin Brown Ale, Potomac IPA, Ashcat Pale Ale, and one notable beer as a tribute to their resident Ghost.... Walter's Spirit.

CHAPTER 4

THE GHOST TOWN

OF BERLIN

MAP OF OLD BERLIN

Shortly after midnight, two men were chatting and porch sitting on South Maryland Avenue on a hot summer Saturday in the early morning hours.. They were engaged in discussing the current events regarding NASCAR racing when, suddenly, one of the men caught a glimpse of something that caught his attention. The man watched a dark shadow figure slowly cross the railroad tracks under the decorative streetlight near Railroad Square. The man was silent for a moment and slowly turned his head and looked at his friend and asked him if he just saw what he had seen. The other man was slow to reply, "If you mean that shadow that just crossed the tracks, then yeah, I saw that."

As stated earlier, Leonard Smith platted Berlin in 1787. The first eight lots sold were recorded in 1789 to Charles Beagle, Joseph West, Jonathon Hillery, Captain James Fenwick (two lots), William Oldham, Joseph Collard, and John Nisewanyer. The 1790 US Census shows several of these landowners residing here in Berlin and current residents live upon that same land that was inhabited so long ago.

The Village of Berlin consisted of three main streets running North to South; First Street, Second Street, and Third Street. These streets are now known as Maple Avenue, Maryland Avenue, and Virginia Avenue, respectfully. These streets ran south, close to the Potomac River and had several streets and alleys running East and West; Railroad Street, Water Street, and High Street, respectfully, with High Street now known as West Potomac Street. The routes in and out of town were Petersville Road, which retraced the Highland Indian Trail, and two county roads leading into and out of town.

As Berlin was settled, most of its citizens were engaged in agriculture, as a fine flouring mill was established here. The Baltimore & Ohio Railroad Company and the Chesapeake and Ohio Canal Company both arrived here in 1834. The village became focused upon the benefits of the C&O Canal as the railroad just ran through on its way to Martinsburg, Virginia. The C&O Canal made it possible to further export the finely milled Berlin flour to Georgetown, just outside of Washington, DC, and all the way west to Cumberland, MD. At the time of the Civil War, the population of Berlin was near three hundred. The economic depression experienced after the Civil War caused that popu-lation to be reduced to around two hundred. Later, the B&O Railroad placed a combination freight and passenger depot here, and the transportation of goods and passengers increased. In the late 1880s, the B&O Railroad Company announced that its main railroad classification yards were to be moved from Martinsburg, VA to Berlin. Then, most everything in the village changed.

Knowing there was confusion in that another Berlin existed in Maryland, just outside of Ocean City, in Worcester County, the B&O Railroad changed Berlin to Brunswick. Within just a few short years, the Railroad built many industrial buildings, laid miles of railroad track, constructed the turntable, built Brunswick's original roundhouse, and opened the new railroad yard. From 1889 to 1891, the population increased tenfold from two hundred residents to two thousand residents. A boomtown emerged as railroad families needed housing, businesses, churches, and organizations.

What we now refer to as "Old Berlin" became the new Brunswick. The original lots platted as Berlin was fully developed, and adjacent land was annexed for the needed growth. Houses began to pop up quickly on what is now Brunswick Street, B Street, C Street, and all the Avenues along the west side of town. Also developed was the land further down East Potomac Street that is now First through Seventh Avenues. What is now known as Downtown Brunswick, the historic main street area located along the pronounced commercial blocks of West and East Potomac Streets, came about by two critical factors; the need to get buildings out of the floodplain and the B&O Railroad's desire to expand its new yard.

This photograph from the archives of the Brunswick Museum shows Brunswick around the year 1893. Besides the bridge in the background, this view wasn't much different from Berlin in 1890. To the right is a large boarding house that is still standing on South Maple Avenue. It is located next to the building that once housed Mommer's Diner. Dr. Horine's Drug Store building replaced the other house to the front right. That intersection is now Brunswick's "Square Corner". The Short Farm, is shown, which is now where the American Legion is located. In the back right, the Opera House is still standing. The Opera House had two commercial storefronts on the ground floor. The crowds' weight in the Opera House on the second level caused the floors to fail, and the property was condemned. To the back left is an old boarding house. The location of this house and the Opera House are now covered with paving and serves as the Maryland   Transit Commuter Parking Lot.

This photo from the Brunswick Heritage Museum shows the railroad crossing into Berlin, circa 1900. The man at the center of the image is standing in what is now South Maryland Avenue. The building to the left is the Berlin Deport. The buildings across the track housed Horine's first drugstore and Blessing's Restaurant. The man on the right shows up in the few Berlin photos that exist, and his job was to stand on the tracks and warn folks of approaching trains. This position was established after 1891 when a young man was hit by a train and his body parts were strewn for 100 feet along the tracks at this very crossing.

Shortly after opening the new Brunswick yard in 1891, the B&O Railroad saw a problem with their plan at Brunswick. Massive steam locomotives had to travel from the west end of town, through the inhabited village towards the newly built turntable and roundhouse on the east end of town. Eventually, the Railroad began a lengthy and turbulent process of attaining all of the land located below High Street (now Potomac Street) to the canal. As buildings were demolished, their materials were recycled into the new buildings being constructed on the higher elevation on High Street (Potomac Street). A few of the Old Berlin buildings were moved, such as the old hotel to Second Street (now North Maryland Avenue). Most of Old Berlin's commercial area is now sealed like a tomb, resting under the Maryland Transit Commuter Parking Lot.

Does this land exhibit paranormal activity? Did the building materials recycled from Old Berlin carry any paranormal energy? Do our former inhabitants of Old Berlin still walk their streets? This author and many paranormal investigators will answer yes to all of those questions. For years these investigators have assembled evidence of interactions with ghostly spirits of Berlin/Brunswick's past. For reasons unknown, these spirts wish to communicate with us. For reasons unknown, we so badly want to communicate with them.

During a paranormal investigation of the Brunswick Museum, members of the Ghost Pit traveled down South Maryland Avenue to the 1920's B&O Railroad caboose that is on display in Railroad Square. This author was lucky to be in attendance. Upon arriving, a gifted psychic medium, Tracie Andrews Cavnar, sensed men standing around the caboose.

She looked at me and said, "I think they are railroad workers trying to fix it and wondering how it got here."

Tracie went on to say that the men were discussing how bad the condition of the caboose was underneath. The men kept telling her how rusted out the undercarriage was. The SLS camera was used, and to everyone's surprise, it mapped out several figures around the caboose.

On a different night, during a return trip to the caboose, an investigator saw the inside of the upper window fog up, in a circle pattern, as if someone was breathing on it from the inside. This window is where a brakeman would ride during the duration of a trip. The fog then slowly dissipated. A strong sense of dedication still drives these railroaders even in the afterlife.

Could one of these workers have been the shadow figure that the men on the porch saw? Could the shadow figure have been just residual energy from someone who crossed the tracks into Berlin so many times, so many years ago?

One spring day, this author was volunteering at the Brunswick Heritage Museum when a young woman rushed into the building eager to have me listen to an EVP she captured. The EVP was a crystal clear but breathy "Rebecca." I complimented the young lady on her "catch" and asked her where she got it. She responded, "The Old Berlin Cemetery."

I froze when I heard her reply, and she could tell I had a disapproving look upon my face. "Why don't you like investigating that cemetery?" she asked. "It seems like such an obvious place to hunt for ghosts.", she said. "The answer is simple.", I replied.

First and foremost, this author believes a spirit would want to return where they lived and worked, perhaps even the place they perished, but, not a cemetery. I went on to preach my sermon regarding the Old Berlin Cemetery.

The Old Berlin Cemetery, also called the Lutheran Cemetery, displays about 25 tombstones. There are most likely about 200 bodies in that cemetery. Who are the people buried there? They are our working class founders of Berlin. During the time our town was called Berlin, if you had wealth, you were buried in Petersville, or you "went back home" to Virginia. The Berlin Cemetery contains farmers, homemakers, canal workers, early railroaders, Civil War veterans, and children who died so young.

One newspaper article stated there was a group of eight Irish Canal workers who died during a pandemic. A local Irishman donated his lot in the Berlin Cemetery for the workers. One hole was opened, and all eight were plopped in and covered. Over the years, the cemetery fell into disrepair. Being no playground on that end of town, children began to use the lot for baseball. Tombstones fell, and no-one fixed them. Monuments started to go missing, and some family members took stones in fear that someone else might steal them.

So why do I not investigate the Old Berlin Cemetery? The answer is simple, the forgotten folks in this cemetery have been disrespected enough, and I leave them alone so these poor souls may have some peace.

This photo from the Brunswick History Commission shows tombstones in the Old Berlin Cemetery.

CHAPTER 5

THE WALLS WHISPER

Many of Brunswick's oldest streets are comprised of homes built for our earliest railroad workers and their families. Once the decision was made in the late 1880s to move the B&O Railroad's main classification yard operation here, many other houses, stores, businesses, churches, and organizations were needed to support future railroad families.

Brunswick is sometimes referred to as a "company town", but the B&O Railroad Company managed housing much differently than their coal company counterparts. The coal mining companies usually owned everything located within an entire town. They charged their employees for every aspect of life within the town, creating the adage "Don't call me St. Peter, cause I can't go. I owe my soul to the company store".

Luckily for our ancestors, the B&O Railroad Company had a completely different philosophy when it came to the subject of housing. Railroad work may have been dangerous, and workers may have died on the job, but they certainly didn't owe their soul to the company.

The B&O Railroad offered to assist workers with the purchase of their building lots and with the construction of their homes. To attract early railroad workers to Berlin, and later Brunswick, the B&O Railroad would deduct your mortgage payment straight from your railroad paycheck. The B&O Railroad employee "owned" the house, and when the house was resold, if it had gained in value or the worker had created equity, the worker collected that equity. In essence, the B&O Railroad invested in their workers and helped them attain wealth that benefited them and their family. This situation was beneficial to the early railroaders as often the B&O Railroad did shuffle its employees along the line. Many of the first Brunswick railroad workers had their positions move to Cumberland, Baltimore, Hagerstown, Martinsburg, and other locations as the Railroad adapted to its growth and development. In 1890, a landowner of thousands of acres annexed into Brunswick offered his lots free of charge as long as his contracting company built the homes. This same builder began a lumber business and a brickyard to support the growth of Brunswick.

This annexed land was once the land the natives traveled, farmland that slaves labored, and land in which Civil War soldiers camped and skirmished.

From the Brunswick History Commission, the photo on the previous page shows the Spitzer home located at Brunswick Street and Delaware Avenue.

From the Brunswick History Commission, this photo shows the Hymes-Hogan House located at North Virginia Avenue and B Street.

When you talk to people who live in some of these oldest homes, located on Brunswick's oldest streets, they begin to recant stories containing a common theme. These residents talk about hearing conversations within their homes. If not, conversations, voices. When the conversations or voices are investigated, it is found that no one is located in the house speaking or conversing.

These muffled voices and conversations are a common occurrence. In physics, the phenomena almost replicates what is known as string theory, where two time periods can blend, and you can hear the conversations of the past and interact.... the walls whisper. For those of you old enough to remember cassette tapes, or even older to remember reel to reel players, think of it as when you recorded over your music so much that the old music bled through into the newer recorded music.

Once, on the Brunswick Heritage Museum's annual Brunswick Ghost and History Walk through downtown Brunswick, this author led a group down a residential street when I stopped the group and explained the phenomena of wall whispers. A middle-aged woman was sitting on her front porch, enjoying a beautiful fall evening where I stopped the group. Overhearing my speech about wall whispers, she interjected herself into the conversation. She apologized for interrupting me but wanted to tell the group that she had heard these shadow conversations in her home. Many times on the Ghost and History walk, residents confirm what is being said or offer their own stories.

This photo, from the Brunswick History Commission, shows the Conway House located at 4 East Potomac Street.

CHAPTER 6

THE ENERGY SOURCE: THE POTOMAC RIVER

Brunswick is lucky to have both the Potomac River, an American Heritage River, and the Chesapeake and Ohio Canal National Historical Park right in its backyard. Both tourism attractions offer many recreational activities to our residents and visitors to the city. Activities such as walking, running, biking, fishing, boating, and even some hunting. The Potomac River is also the main source for the City of Brunswick's drinking water supply. The Potomac River is truly the reason Brunswick is located where it is today. As the Potomac River is so vital to us today, it was also vital to those who lived here in the past.

The Potomac River is about three and a half million years old. In 1608, Captain John Smith explored the Potomac River. He came into contact with the first people here, the Susquehannock, who were part of the Algonquin alliance. Susquehannock is Algonquin for "people of the muddy river".[2] The Native people called this river the "Patawomeck". The Natives knew the Potomac River was important. It was so important that the territory was worth fighting other tribes and dying to have unlimited access to the Potomac's water. The Potomac River offered our natives many different fish species, including eels, that provided needed protein to feed and sustain the native tribe. When the Potomac Riverbanks overflowed, the muddy river water provided nutrients to plants. These plants were used for food, providing fruits and grains that were needed for the native people. The Potomac River's water and plants also lured other protein to the natives. Animals such as deer, turkeys, bears, and yes, even bison. The Potomac River also provided a navigational route through Susquehannock territory.

As local author and historian, Don Peterson states in his study, "Native American Fish Traps in the Potomac River, Brunswick, MD", Native Americans were born, raised families, died, and were buried in the Brunswick area for the last twelve thousand years. "White men" have resided here for about three hundred years. Little evidence

---

[2] https://www.legendsofamerica.com/susquehannock-tribe/

is left from our native peoples, but they left some evidence of their existence to find if luck is on our side and we look hard enough.

Many Brunswick area residents find arrowheads and other Native American artifacts in their yards. Some artifacts are found while planting flowers or perhaps while walking along one of the city's numerous eroding creek beds, as the Susquehannock were creek dwellers. Most of these arrow points were not used in battles but for hunting or spearing fish. Smaller points were for hunting birds; thus, they are called "bird points". This author was blessed in finding an ax head in a Brunswick garden once. Pottery shards, some decorative, have been found in Brunswick area fields after annual plowing.

An unconcealed display of evidence that proves our native ancestors were here has been right in front of our eyes for hundreds of years. Let's look at the rock formations in the Potomac River that were once used as fish traps. These fish traps are sporadically placed along the Potomac River within the greater Brunswick area. Constructed in "V" shaped formations, the traps' purpose was to force the fish to the small angle where fish baskets were placed to catch the fish.

According to Peterson, the fishing event required many people to accomplish because the basket needed to be removed and replaced with another one. The fish were then transported to the shore to be processed and dried for winter storage.

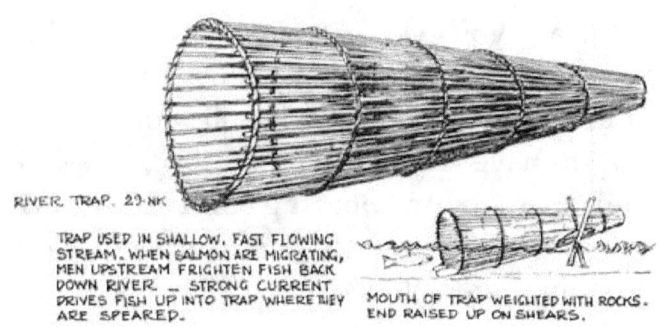

RIVER TRAP. 29-NK

TRAP USED IN SHALLOW, FAST FLOWING STREAM. WHEN SALMON ARE MIGRATING, MEN UPSTREAM FRIGHTEN FISH BACK DOWN RIVER — STRONG CURRENT DRIVES FISH UP INTO TRAP WHERE THEY ARE SPEARED.

MOUTH OF TRAP WEIGHTED WITH ROCKS. END RAISED UP ON SHEARS.

This illustration shows the basket placed in the angle of the "V" formation of Native American fish traps found along the Potomac River.

After the natives were driven out of the area, this land was settled by Europeans. These settlers were attracted to this area for the same reasons the first peoples were; water, food, and navigation. As the settlers found the native people's fish traps, they too used them for fishing. They also used the conveniently stacked stones as foundations of the earliest homes here.

Spiritual History

The native peoples were very spiritual and often prayed to their gods. They believed in elementals such as earth, wind, air, rain, and fire.

Have you ever walked along the canal and felt that someone is watching you? Do you think the spirits of the native people still protect their land? EVP's have been recorded in Brunswick that contains drum beating and unidentifiable languages. Are Brunswick's first peoples trying to communicate with us?

Paranormal Theory

It has been a long-standing paranormal theory that running water is a conductor for paranormal activity. Many towns along and near the Potomac River are rumored to host haunted activity. Towns like Shepherdstown, Harpers Ferry, and Charlestown in West Virginia.

In 2009, author and researcher Sharon Day visited fifty well known haunted locations throughout the United States. Her goal was to note common features that these sites shared. One of the most common shared features was water. Forty-one of the fifty places she visited were near water sources.[3] This author often presents the theory that the Potomac River is undoubtedly a conduit for most paranormal activity within Brunswick and Knoxville.

Brunswick's Creature

One spring, in the 1980s two men, traveled to the Potomac River island, right off the Brunswick shore, in between the states of Maryland and Virginia. It was an early Sunday morning. The weather was clear and beautiful, a bit chilly, but the temperature would soon increase. A day of fishing was the plan for the day as both men worked hard as carpenters for a local construction company, and both men could use a day to relax, drink some beer, and fish for catfish.

They landed on the small island and pushed their boat firmly upon the sandy soil. They unloaded their gear and began to walk to the other edge of the island. It was one of their favorite fishing spots along this area of the Potomac. As

---

[3]http://www.ghosthuntingtheories.com/2015/05/water-as-paranormal-conduit.html

they got near their desired fishing location, the men began to smell a horrible foul smell.

A putrid smell that they later described as a decaying animal mixed with the smell of rotting eggs. Both men feared they were about to find a decomposing body on the island. They thought perhaps a boat capsized and a fisherman drowned in the Potomac River, and the body washed up on the island's shore. The water level was a bit high due to numerous recent rain events. When they walked through some tall grass, the men found just what was causing such the foul stench.

An ape-like creature was crouched around a dead deer. To their horror, it was feasting upon the animal's flesh, using both enormous hands to shove raw meat into its mouth. It was eating as if it had not had food in some time. When the creature stood up, it was a bit taller than an average human and was hairy with brown hair, much like an ape. The men gasped, and the "Ape Man" heard them. The creature turned towards them and let out a roar that stuck absolute terror into the men. It was then that the men noticed the creature's muscular features in both its upper body and legs.

Without hesitation, the men dropped most of their gear and ran like the wind towards their boat. To their horror, the men could hear the creature running fast behind them making sounds as it ran. Adrenaline fueled their sprint to the edge of the island. As they approached the boat, the first man sprung forward and jumped inside. Luckily, his forward momentum shifted the boat from the sand and into the water. The second man seeing the boat was now in the water, pushed the boat from behind at least six or seven more steps into the river, and jumped inside, never losing his stride. Both men grabbed a paddle and were paddling fast towards the Brunswick shore. The man at the front of the boat could not bring himself to look back towards the beast. Looking back, the other man saw only the rear of the creature as if it reached the island's edge and gave up chase due to the water.

The men reached Brunswick, loaded up their boat, and quickly left town. Smelling a horrible smell in their pickup truck, one man noticed that the other had soiled his jeans during the horrific event. Both men, to this day, have never returned to go fishing in Brunswick. That dear readers is the story of the Brunswick's Bigfoot.

A Sight Too Awful

It was in the early 1930s when a man named Robert drove his automobile down South Maryland Avenue, heading towards the edge of the Potomac River in Brunswick. He unloaded his boat and was excited for a relaxing day of fishing. A relaxing day of fishing, however, wasn't in store for our Robert. He wasn't on the water long before something caught his eye that looked odd in the river. He paddled close to the object, paddling right up beside it to take a look. When he looked, he quickly turned to the other side of the boat and vomited into the river.

He paddled back to shore and ran uphill to the B&O Railroad Hospital attached to the Brunswick B&O Railroad YMCA. He ran into the hospital and reported what he saw to the doctor there on duty. After the doctor listened to Robert, he telephoned the hospital in Frederick. He requested for a coroner to be dispatched to Brunswick. The doctor then called the Brunswick police to report a crime.

About an hour later, Robert, the coroner, the doctor, and a Brunswick policeman are all in the boat heading to where Robert saw this horrible sight. The group was a bit uncomfortable in the boat, as Robert was of a stocky build. When they arrive at the location, the policeman finds a thick, brown rope in the water. As he tugs the cord, up surfaces an opalescent, waterlogged, blob of an infant baby girl with the rope tied around her neck and the other end connected to a tree.

In a small town such as Brunswick, an infant girl's recovery from the Potomac River was major news. The local newspapers ran headlines asking residents if their neighbors had a baby, but the baby had not been seen. They also asked residents if they knew of any women who were expecting but now they were not, and there was no child to be found. The Brunswick police begged anyone who knew anything of this crime to please come forward and contact them. The crime went unsolved. The deed was explained as a despicable way to hide a child born out of wedlock or due to the great depression, a parent or parents couldn't afford to take care of the child and disposed of her in the river.

A very generous and sympathetic person in Brunswick donated their cemetery lot. Today, there stands a small gravestone in the shape of a lamb for "Baby Jane", as in Jane Doe, the infant girl found in the Potomac River at Brunswick, Maryland. The story, however, doesn't end there.

Many local duck hunters enter the Potomac River at Brunswick. Sometimes in the early morning hours, these hunters report hearing a baby cry. A bobcat, at times, makes a sound sounds like a crying baby, but these experienced hunters know what a bobcat sounds like. These hunters swear what they hear is a baby crying.

Are the faint cries being heard along the Potomac River in Brunswick from the ghost of our little Baby Jane or are the cringing cries coming from the poor soul of another baby submerged in the Potomac River, abandoned, hoping to be found one day? Are the cries just a figment of these hunter's imagination? One can only speculate.

CHAPTER 7

THE CIVIL WAR

One bright summer day, this author received a call from a lady living in Brunswick who wished to share her ghost story with me. Just a few nights prior to our phone call she awoke thirsty and walked to her kitchen sink to draw a glass of water. A window was located at the sink that overlooked her side yard. She looked out the window while enjoying a refreshing drink of Brunswick tap water from her glass. She was surprised to see what she said looked like two men sitting at a campfire in her side yard. She described the men as wearing uniforms but really couldn't tell me anything else about how they looked. She said she stared for a few seconds and noticed that the men were "foggy", almost mist-like. The ethereal men and the fire then slowly dissipated like blowing into thin air.

Although a bit shaken, she went out her side door to look for the men but found no one there and no sign of the campfire. She did note that she could faintly smell burning wood, but that could have been coming from the closely located Brunswick Family Campground. Often, the summer breeze coming off the Potomac River carries the smell of burning campfires from the campground through Brunswick. I asked if I could visit her house to investigate the location, and she allowed me to do so.

The next day, when I arrived at her house, the very nice lady eagerly greeted me. She showed me the site on her property where she saw the ghostly apparitions. When looking at the yard, I immediately noticed a depression in the ground as if the earth had been disturbed in the past. I thought to myself that the site could have been an outhouse at one time because the location was about 30 feet from the side door.

However, the home was newer, so it would have been built with inside plumbing. Perhaps an older house sat on the site? I also noticed a stream bed in the back yard that was possibly providing a paranormal energy conduit to this property. I asked if it would be possible for me to come back with my metal detector. A brief hesitation and a promise from me that my goal was not to bulldoze her yard, she agreed to my request.

Twenty minutes later, a resounding beep comes from my detector as I passed over the yard's dip. I dug a plug from the ground and out came a tiny piece of metal later identified as a small bit belonging to a Civil War-era boot spur. But the most exciting thing I found was still left in the ground, corroborating evidence of this lady's ghost story......burnt wood from a long-ago extinguished campfire. As the house was modern, it is assumed that these soldiers camped near the stream bed during the Civil War. For whatever reason, these apparitions can still be seen camping here.

You may be wondering why Civil War soldiers? What role did Berlin play in this war, and why does it matter today?

Berlin's Unknown Civil War History

Berlin's important role during the Civil War is the most unknown historical fact among Brunswick's current population. This fact can be attributed to two main factors. First, there were no major battles fought here. Second, there are few relatives here presently from when Brunswick was Berlin. Most original Berlin families moved away from the area after the B&O Railroad decided to move its main yard operation. Many of these families preferred the slower, agricultural lifestyle than the more urban area that Brunswick was becoming. When these families moved out of the area, they took their memories and stories of Berlin's history with them, including accounts of what happened here during the Civil War.

Before the Civil War, Petersville area farms, which Berlin was a part of, used enslaved African American labor to cultivate crops, mostly wheat for flour. In 1861, an inevitable war was on most Berliners' minds since the village bordered the south on the Potomac River's other side. An excellent, new, covered bridge spanned the Potomac River here. Placed upon stone pillars, the bridge was completed around 1858 to the delight of local farmers from both Maryland and Virginia. They bartered crops and other needed goods with each other.

An order from Confederate General Robert E. Lee was given to Thomas Jackson, later known as "Stonewall" Jackson, to destroy the Bridges spanning the Potomac at Berlin and Point of Rocks in Maryland, and the bridge at Harpers Ferry in Virginia (now West Virginia). Lee postulated that the bridges' burning was necessary to protect the confederacy from an easy attack by the Northern Army.

The orders were obeyed, and on an early morning in June of 1861, the new bridge was covered in coal oil and peppered with gunpowder. The bridge was then lit on fire, and the blaze lit the sky as if it were noon. The citizens of Berlin gathered and watched the bridge burn. The reality of the Civil War just arrived for the residents of Berlin.

What made the little village of Berlin crucial during the Civil War was its proximity to the B&O Railroad and the Potomac River. Needed supplies were delivered to Berlin by rail. Numerous messages were sent by telegraph via the B&O Railroad's telegraph poles and wires. Our Berlin had the distinction of twice being the location of the Headquarters of the Army of the Potomac, once after the battle of Sharpsburg/Antietam, and once after the battle of Gettysburg. Both times, pontoon bridges were placed across the Potomac River for the Union Army to chase the Confederates as they fled south.

After the battle of Sharpsburg/Antietam, the

number of wounded was so large that soldiers were placed on trains and cared for in Berlin and Knoxville. The Union dead were buried here in temporary graves until select units came and dug the bodies and removed them to Sharpsburg. Numerous local homes and churches were used as "hospitals" to nurse the wounded. During the war, many soldiers were stationed in Berlin to protect the railroad tracks from sabotage.

This photo is an Alexander Gardener print from the National Archives. The photo shows Berlin after the battle of Gettysburg. A Union infantry unit is crossing the pontoon bridge into the South to give chase to the retreating confederate rebels.

Where Past & Present Meet

An interesting myth passed down for generations in Brunswick is the nonexistent experience of "Brick Yard Hill". Brick Yard Hill is located on Second Avenue. It is a steep slope that countless children have enjoyed sled riding down during winter snowstorms. The name stems from a local businessman, Charles M. Wenner, who sold his land for building lots. He began a lumber yard and created a brickyard during the Brunswick building boom of 1890. The brickyard was located off of what is now Second Avenue.

For decades, people have stopped their vehicles at the bottom of the hill, on the flat, placed their vehicles in neutral, and claim to experience the phenomena of having their automobile pushed up Brick Yard Hill. The theory presented is that the ghosts of Union soldiers, stationed here in the past, push your vehicle up the hill as they would have pushed cannons. As an important reminder, this author would like to state that stopping your vehicle in a traveled portion of a roadway and placing that vehicle in neutral is not suggested and **you should not do it**. Take the story as a myth, fictionalized using facts regarding Berlin's storied Civil War past.

The Clock Chimed Twelve

One Brunswick home that was used as a Civil War hospital after the battle of Antietam / Sharpsburg is still standing today. In the 1970s, an elderly widow lived in the old home. It was her descendants who originally built the house and lived there during the Civil War. A local woman who lived just a few blocks away took on the dutiful task of checking in on the frail octogenarian, at the very least, once a week.

On one of these check-ins, the visiting woman was invited in for lunch. As the two ladies sat at the kitchen table discussing their weekly updates and enjoying cucumber sandwiches with hot tea, a grandfather clock deeply rang. The visitor stopped her conversation and slowly counted the chiming of the clock. Ten......Eleven....... Twelve times. Looking down at her wristwatch, she confirmed that it was indeed noon. "What a lovely deep chime that grandfather clock has", said the visiting woman.

The elderly homeowner in the middle of a sip of tea slowly swallowed and agreed. Shaking slightly more than usual, she answered, "It is, and it chimes often." She continued by saying, "But....there is one issue with it, dear." She looked at the younger woman as she finished her thought , saying, "There is no clock that chimes in this house."

Astonished at the statement, the guest asked if she could look around for a clock and was even more baffled when after visiting each room, not one chiming clock was found.

It was forty years later when a new family was living in the same home, not knowing of any previous paranormal activity there, reached out to me to discuss abnormal activity in the same house. No chiming clocks were reported this time, but the house did show signs of paranormal activity.

A prevalent theme within these local Civil War- era homes is repeating sounds that take place daily, or nightly always at the same time. This is known as a residual haunting. These hauntings are not intelligent hauntings, meaning the spirits will not communicate with you. Instead, these spirits act as if they are on a repetitive timeline, reliving the same daily tasks, often mundane, they partook in when they were alive. Examples of these activities include walking up and down steps, getting up from a kitchen table, and even jogging on a path. It is believed that these spirits are not conscious. Instead, they are an imprint of energy within the area.

One instance of this phenomenon was reported to this author by a person who lived in Downtown Brunswick in a house that existed during the Civil War. He was a young man of about twenty-four and had a muscular build. He told me that each night around midnight, the sounds of boots with spurs climb up the stairs. I asked what this young, muscular man did when he heard the steps. "Did you run to the door and open it?", I excitedly asked. "Did you see what was at the top of the steps?", I followed up. "No man, I pulled the covers over my head until the sounds of the steps went away.", he answered.

Did the horrible activity here during the Civil War leave an imprint on Brunswick's timeline? Are soldiers from the war still on duty here? Do they still camp here every night? Is the campfire smoke you smell really from the Brunswick Campground or the smoke from a campfire from so long ago? Are these soldiers trying to communicate with us, or are their souls just reliving their daily routines each day and night?

CHAPTER 8

THE B&O RAILROAD

The previous chapters of this book have slowly added ingredients for a tasty haunted location recipe for Brunswick. We have taken a water source and added our Native American history and Civil War history into the mixing bowl. Now comes one of our final ingredients to be added: the Baltimore & Ohio Railroad's dangerous working conditions.

One Saturday evening, a paranormal team was investigating the Brunswick Heritage Museum. The small group, like many paranormal teams, had a member who is a psychic medium. This team has an operating procedure in which the psychic medium explores the location first and then shares what they sensed, with only one team member to validate the team's findings at the end of the investigation. This step is essential so as not to sway investigators into biased investigating.

The psychic medium came down from upstairs and requested that this author enter a room for a side conversation. "I turned the corner on the second floor, and there was an African American man in bib overalls and a work hat there.", said the medium.

"Really?", I asked.

"Yes, and he's outraged!", she proclaimed.

"What is he angry about?", I asked.

"He's stuck here in the Museum Building (he called the building the Eagles Club) and can't get to his engine.", she answered.

"He's going to be late.", she said.

She went on to tell me the ghost mentioned his locomotive engine number. I wrote the engine number down in my notepad. After a brief web search, low and behold, the locomotive engine number provided was from a B&O Railroad locomotive engine in service from around 1900 until the early 1940s.

As mentioned earlier in the book, after prohibition, the Red Men sold the building to the Brunswick Eagles Club, and the Eagles operated there until the late 1960s. Taking all this information into consideration determined that our resident spirit on the second floor, the floor now known as Eagles Hall, worked on the B&O Railroad here in Brunswick during the 1930s and 1940s.

I presented this information to the psychic medium and requested that if she could "tap" into this gentleman again, ask him why he was here. Near the end of the investigation, the medium requested I meet her on the second floor. Smiling, she pronounced, "I have a name for you." She gave me the name of the worker, which I immediately recognized as a former Brunswick railroader.

"So why is he here?", I inquired.

"His picture is on the wall here, and he says that everyone knows him.", she answered.

"He likes it here because there are many other Brunswick railroaders in and out of this building.", she concluded.

Do the railroad artifacts and photos exhibited in the Museum hold onto residual energy from those that once held onto them? Does displaying artifacts in the museum that once belonged to people of the past attract those same people to visit the Museum? Is there a camaraderie among deceased Brunswick railroaders that they enjoy visiting each other at the Brunswick Heritage Museum?

The Railroad Arrives

As stated earlier, the B&O Railroad's presence here dates back to 1834 when the original lines were laid in Berlin as the B&O Railroad continued to Martinsburg, Virginia. We don't know much about those earliest track layers in Berlin except that they were most likely African Americans. These first track workers were called "Gandy Dancers", because they worked in rhythm to lay the tracks and hammer spikes much like a prison chain gang would. Most of the songs were either religious or raunchy, and sometimes a mixture of both. The music not only allowed the men to work in unison but also soothed the soul as the work was hard, and the workdays were long. These workers were free men, but the B&O Railroad worked them more than 10-12 hours per day.

The earliest workers in Berlin formed a small section gang. This "gang" of workers was responsible for maintaining the railroad tracks within a specific section, Brunswick to Weverton, for example. It was not until the B&O Railroad decided to move its main yard here in the late 1880s that the number of Railroad employees here swelled in large numbers.

Work at a Price

Since the very day B&O Railroad workers stuck a shovel into the ground to work on the yard, injuries and death surrounded workers. Railroad work is inherently dangerous. Even more so before labor unions pushed for improved technology and safety enhancements to be put into place. Before the yards even opened, a prominent young man, David Taylor, lost his life in a terrible accident.

A SAD ACCIDENT.

A Young Man Killed at the Berlin Railroad Yard.

David J. Taylor was struck by train No. 10, going East, at the new yard of the B. & O. Railroad, Berlin, this county, last evening and instantly killed. The train whilst going East was running on and occupying the west-bound track, hence the accident. Mr. Taylor was 19 years old and was one of the most promising and interesting young men of Berlin. He was working on the new yard at the time the accident occurred. The scene of the accident is about 500 yards east of the village. Taylor was an industrious and attentive workman and his horrible death is deeply regretted by all who knew him.

Many injuries to Brunswick railroad workers were caused by using a "link and pin" system of coupling cars together. The illustration on the opposite page demonstrates the operation. These processes required a railroad worker to stand in between two substantial railroad cars, weighing thousands of pounds when empty, that he had no control over. As the cars got closer to each other, the workers had to reach in with their hands and place a pin into the coupler to latch them together. This process left a lot of room for error, and those errors caused many hands to be smashed, fingers to be lost, body parts to be amputated, and caused workers to be smashed to death in between cars. Since the purpose of the large yards in Brunswick was to make up trains, these accidents were a common, daily occurrence.

A "PICNIC."

A "Picnic"? This work was most likely not a "picnic". The previous illustration shows another dangerous job for early Brunswick railroaders employed as brakemen on the B&O Railroad. In all kinds of weather, brakemen had to climb on top of railroad cars to turn the hand brakes manually. Often these workers slipped off the cars and were crushed by the moving trains.

Heroes in White Coats

Injuries and death were such a common occurrence for railroad workers in Brunswick that the B&O Railroad employed physicians and nursing staff on its payroll here. Brunswick physicians who treated patients for the B&O Railroad included Dr. Arlington Horine, Dr. Levin West, Dr. J.W. Hilleary, Dr. Harry Hedges, and Dr. Charles Crum. When amputations of limbs were needed, these physicians called upon doctors in neighboring communities for assistance. As the number of work-related injuries increased, a hospital annex was added to the existing B&O RR YMCA. To date, the number of local injured and dead railroaders total multiple digit thousands. Not hundreds, but thousands of people.

The B&O Railroad Emergency Hospital staff was not limited to treating railroad workers. The hospital staff often treated children in the Brunswick school system, providing services to the students, such as physical examinations and immunizations against diseases. The hospital staff also treated the general public when called upon regarding events that created general health concerns like when they treated patients during the Spanish Flu pandemic of 1918. The B&O Railroad knew the general health and well-being of the town residents reflected upon the railroad's health and well-being.

This photo is from the Brunswick Heritage Museum and shows the nursing staff at the B&O Railroad Emergency Hospital that was attached to the B&O RR YMCA in Brunswick.

Another dangerous aspect of railroad work was the occurrence of train derailments. These train wrecks were very common in Brunswick's early history. Railroad tracks needed to be correctly maintained to keep the trains and cars upon the tracks. Speed was often a factor in these accidents as railroad management expected trains to run on time even if the crew began their journey late or fell behind during travel. The concept of "making up time" was not only encouraged but, in many cases, ordered. The results were often disastrous and deadly. Photos of wrecked steam locomotives demonstrate how massive this equipment was compared to the size of a human. Train wrecks were such a common occurrence that the B&O Railroad employed workers solely clearing wrecks from the tracks. These wreck crews equipped with large cranes called wreckers would be dispatched to quickly remove damaged equipment from the tracks to resume freight and passengers' movement.

The photo on the opposite page is from the author's collection. The image shows a wreck on the B&O Railroad line from Brunswick to Knoxville. The photo dates from the 1910s-1920s.

One train wreck story, very personal to this author, is one I have never placed in print.

I had a store in Downtown Brunswick during the 1990s. I carried railroad memorabilia, among other antiques and collectibles. Many railroaders collect railroad memorabilia, and one who did would often visit me weekly at my store. We became friends, and these weekly visits and chats lasted for a few years. He was a passenger engineer on a local run and would stay at the Motel Sleepers / Green Country Inn, which had rooms reserved for railroad workers, much like the YMCA did. This engineer would catch a ride down to the Brunswick yard early then walk up into town before his run.

One snowy day, I was contemplating whether to open or not due to the weather conditions. I thought of my weekly visitor and opened the shop. I thought he wasn't going to visit this particular day as I heard the bell on my door ring and in popped his head. I can still see and hear him as he proclaimed, "I'm short on time, so I can't visit." He then popped his head out of the door and walked on down the street. Later in the day, the fatal Silver Spring train crash of 1996 occurred, killing eight passengers and three MARC crew members, including my weekly visitor.

BRAKEMAN KILLED IN BRUNSWICK YARD.

J. O. Grimley, Aged 22, Crushed to Death Between His Engine and a Car.

J. O. Grimsley [spelled two ways], aged 22, a native of Shenandoah City, Va., and a brakeman on the Cumberland Division of the B. & O. Railroad, was killed last Sunday morning in the west-bound yards at Brunswick, this valley, by being crushed between the engine and a box car. It is claimed that his death was caused by carelessness of another employe in not locking a switch and also by Grimsley's disregard in entering a switch where there was no light. He was brakeman on the rear of an engine and was struck before he could jump. His grip upon his engine was so tight that even after life was extinct, his hand had to be pried loose. His left arm was torn off. He had been on the railroad less than one year and consequently was not a member of the Brotherhood of Trainmen.

Did the energy left during these horrible deaths leave an imprint in Brunswick? Are many fatalities the reason so many railroaders visit the Brunswick Heritage Museum and other Brunswick landmarks?

CHAPTER 9

THE MOST HAUNTED STREET IN BRUNSWICK

Whenever this author informs the public that I investigate the paranormal realm, they usually respond with two questions. Ironically, both questions are closely related.

Question Number One

The first question is always, "How did you get started in investigating the paranormal?" The answer is quite lengthy.

As a young child, I was always inquisitive. I would open every drawer of every piece of furniture in addition to opening each door in the house and peeked into every closet for any old things I could find. I always asked questions about the items I would discover. I also began reading the daily newspapers at a young age alternating between reading the newspaper and watching

Saturday morning cartoons.

One Saturday morning, reading the local newspaper, I happened upon a story about a house in Maryland on Keep Tryst Road in Knoxville (in Washington County) being haunted. I vaguely remember the details of the story. I think it included seeing the apparition of a young girl who died on the property a long time ago and seeing the apparition of someone riding a horse on the property. Well, after reading the article, this ten -year-old wanted to hunt for ghosts.

Later that day, we traveled from Knoxville to Brunswick for our weekly shopping trip. As I entered the J.J. Newberry's Five and Dime Store, I walked across the old creaky wooden floors and down the slanted slope, bypassing my customary visit to the toy aisle. I wasn't interested in toys today. Besides, the older woman who worked in the upper office always yelled at me for playing with the toys. Nope, no toys for me; I went straight for where the reading glasses and dime store novels were located. I studiously searched for what I was looking for, and then I swiftly grabbed what I thought I needed to hunt ghosts........ a magnifying glass.

I confidently headed up to the front counter, traveling back up the sloped wooden floor and, told Ms. Rosie, one of our neighbors from Knoxville, that I needed this special magnifying glass because I was going to search for ghosts. She looked down at my purchase with a confused look upon her face and asked if the ghosts I was searching for needed to be magnified. I remained silent, thinking that she just wasn't up to date on this subject as I was. I think the total was a dollar or some small amount, and I paid in change that I had found earlier at my house and kept.

Later that day, we went to eat dinner at the Cindy Dee Diner, as we often did on Saturdays. This location is now home to the Guide House Grill. We usually only dined out once a week, if we ever dined out at all. When I was younger, if we went out to dinner, Saturday meals were consumed at the Cindy Dee Diner. Later, when Frederick stores opened on Sundays, post-church meals found us at Watson's Family Restaurant in Frederick. I enjoyed these two places very much as they offered an experience other than dining at home. Watson's Family Restaurant was decorated with old Frederick memorabilia, which helped fuel my love for local historical artifacts. I would quickly finish my meal before everyone else at the table and then look at all the cool artifacts.

The Cindy Dee Diner was always a dark and mysterious place to me. The restaurant was not necessarily the cleanest diner I ever dined at. The booths each having a jukebox unit that played music at your table. I remember these units were usually always smeared by greasy fingers. Greasy fingers most likely used to eat the popular fried chicken served there. The normal customer base here was used to listening to classic country music, so our table received many stares this day as my sister, and I played "Swingin" by John Anderson. I spent many hours playing the tabletop model of the Pac-Man/Galaxia arcade game. The Delmonico steaks were served sizzling on metal plates, and rainbow trout was served with the head still attached, looking back at me as I looked at it. I was sad when that diner closed.

The route back home to Knoxville Road took us down Keep Tryst Road. I grew excited as I realized we were going to pass the same 'haunted house" I read about that morning in the newspaper. I begged my father to drive my grandparents' silver Buick slowly as we passed the house so I could get a good look at it. As we slowly crept by the house, everyone in the car looked for ghosts including me, as I had my magnifying glass up to one eye and had the other eye closed. I didn't see anything at the house, but everyone else in the car said they saw a ghost, but I knew they were mocking my interest in the subject.

Later, while a student at Brunswick Middle School, I would rush to the school library in the morning, before class began and check out a book on ghosts. I would take the book home and read it at night before I went to sleep. Arriving the next day at school, I would return the book to the library and quickly check out another book. Lurking into the paranormal area was then viewed as odd behavior. Most adults considered any interest beyond a curiosity as "an odd" activity. And then...... Well, that was it. Middle School turned into High School, and as normal for most teenagers, my interests changed.

Sometime around the year 2004, the television show "Ghost Hunters" aired, and it revived my curiosity in the paranormal. Numerous other popular paranormal television shows soon followed that television show. Then, all of a sudden, people lurking into the realm of the supernatural wasn't so odd anymore. All the cool kids were doing it. Teams were formed, websites were created, and societies were established, not clubs or groups but societies.

So then, there I was, an adult interested in Brunswick history and ghost hunting, a popular pastime. That is when it happened, these two worlds collided. Volunteering at the Brunswick Heritage Museum one Sunday, a person who was "ghost hunting" captured an EVP and wanted my take on the recording's historical relevance. The captured EVP was "Carman". The young ghost hunter figured it was someone's name and wanted to know the Museum building's history to see if someone named Carman had worked there or had any history being in the building or involved with the Museum. I informed him that "Carman" was a railroad occupation, a person who worked on railroad cars. That was the historical relevance of his EVP and the building it was captured in. He thanked me for the information I provided. He was off on his way, happily knowing the historical context of his EVP. It was at that very moment I knew I could partake in this paranormal investigating activity as well. Even better, I had the historical knowledge to put my findings into their proper historical context.

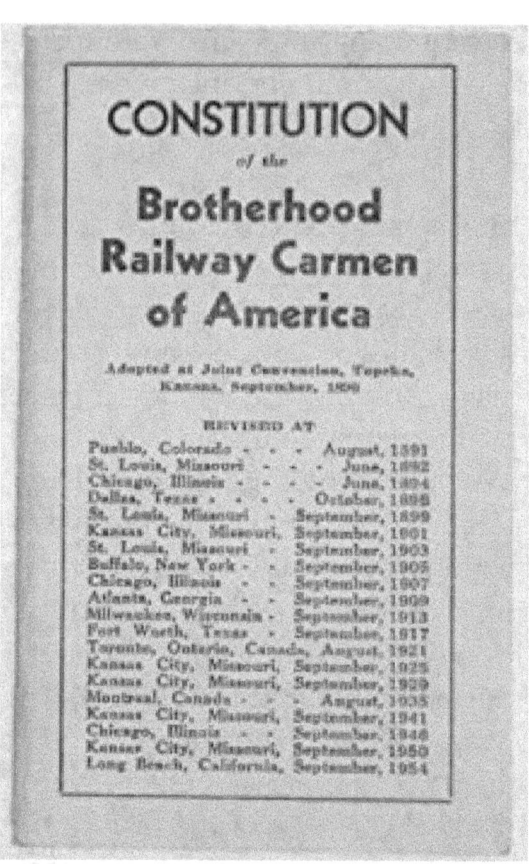

CONSTITUTION
of the
Brotherhood
Railway Carmen
of America

Adapted at Joint Convention, Topeka,
Kansas, September, 1890

REVISED AT

Pueblo, Colorado · · · August, 1891
St. Louis, Missouri · · · June, 1892
Chicago, Illinois · · · · June, 1894
Dallas, Texas · · · · October, 1896
St. Louis, Missouri · September, 1899
Kansas City, Missouri, September, 1901
St. Louis, Missouri · September, 1903
Buffalo, New York · · September, 1905
Chicago, Illinois · · September, 1907
Atlanta, Georgia · · September, 1909
Milwaukee, Wisconsin · September, 1913
Fort Worth, Texas · September, 1917
Toronto, Ontario, Canada, August, 1921
Kansas City, Missouri, September, 1925
Kansas City, Missouri, September, 1929
Montreal, Canada · · · August, 1935
Kansas City, Missouri, September, 1941
Chicago, Illinois · · September, 1946
Kansas City, Missouri, September, 1950
Long Beach, California, September, 1954

Question Number Two

Question number two is always, "What is the most haunted street in Brunswick?"

The answer to this question has taken me years of research to answer. Over the last ten years, many residents have reported to this author paranormal activity that has taken place in their homes or businesses. What do I do with that information? I create a file on each location and maintain a map where I place a mark on the haunted site. I can tell you there is one street in particular where eighty percent of the paranormal activity reported to me occurs in Brunswick. All of the required ingredients for tasty hauntings on this street have been covered in this book's previous chapters.

The **first** ingredient is an area where natives roamed their land. The **second** is that the area was also once a wheat field maintained by enslaved labor. The **third** ingredient is the fact the area has Civil War skirmish history. Soldiers traveled along a creek bed there and used the creek as a source for drinking water. Speaking of the creek bed, it supplies the conduit for paranormal activity, another needed ingredient.

And the **last** ingredient is **railroaders**. The homes of railroaders and their families adorn this older street. Put all of these ingredients together, and you have one large hotspot tasty cake for paranormal activity here in Brunswick.

This street has provided so much paranormal activity. Once, a man who lives on this street told me that he awoke to a man's apparition in uniform riding on horseback through his bedroom. This same apparition has appeared numerous times. The phantom most likely is of a soldier from the Civil War.

A woman who lived on this street told me of the countless times a previous homeowner would be seen standing on the Victorian stairway, staring at her. She eventually moved away. This street has had reports of men camping in a yard, campfire smells, the apparition of a man in a top hat strolling on the sidewalk, a prior female house occupant roaming the summer kitchen, and the list of paranormal activity on this particular street goes on and on.

Does one wonder how many paranormal events have happened on this street that this author doesn't know? Perhaps other areas are just as active, and the activity is not discussed. Please don't be disappointed, dear reader, that this author failed to name the most haunted street in Brunswick, as I have promised many folks over the years that I would not disclose the location of their haunted activity.

CHAPTER 10

ALWAYS VIGILANT

Many years ago, this author owned a business in historic downtown Brunswick. One associated task of owning a business in a small town is networking. At that time, the local Economic Development Commission sponsored monthly business breakfasts as networking events.

At one such business breakfast, I happened to be standing next to the Chief. Another local business owner approached the Chief and eagerly informed him of how pleased he was that officers were checking the doors at night in the historic business district. The Police Chief thanked him for the compliment and stated that he would let the officer know that their efforts were appreciated.

The following month another business breakfast was held. I again was standing near the Chief of Police when he approached the business owner he spoke to at the last month's breakfast. The Chief was puzzled and stated that he wanted to thank the officer who displayed great community policing by checking on the business doors at night during the monthly departmental meeting. To his surprise, not one officer stated that they walked the downtown area, checking on businesses at night. He asked the local businessman for a description of the officer. The business owner closed his eyes and described the officer as male, wearing a hat, twirling his nightstick, and whistling while he checked on doors. The Police Chief looked perplexed as rarely did his officers wear their official hats. They were certainly not allowed to pull out their batons unless they were needed for self-defense.

It was a hot summer day in June of 1909. Like every summer, the carnival had come to Brunswick. At that time, the Brunswick carnival was held in the field located across from the present-day City Park Building on East Potomac Street. Children enjoyed rides on the large mechanical equipment. Adults were eating food from the local churches while catching up with their neighbors. Everyone was enjoying a great time. But unfortunately, a few teenagers were again causing trouble. These teens entertained themselves by sneaking onto the carnival's merry go round without paying to do so. The teens did this so often that the operator of the ride complained to the carnival manager. The carnival manager then complained to the Brunswick policeman on duty at the carnival, Officer William Orrison.

Officer Orrison approached the boys who were often causing trouble around town. The boys shouted profanities at the officer and then ran. However, Officer Orrison was able to grab one of the boys, a Brunswick teenager, aged fifteen. Officer Orrison placed the teen under arrest and began to walk him to the magistrate's office to charge him with theft. On their way to the Magistrate's office, the two walked past the boy's home, where a crowd came out of the house and surrounded Officer Orrison. Officer Orrison did his best to calm the mob, but tempers overtook the group, and the crowd began to beat and kick the officer. During the scuffle, one of the mob members grabbed Officer Orrison's nightstick and beat him until he was unconscious. Officer Orrison never woke up and died upon the dirt street in

Brunswick.

There were witnesses to the crime, and a suspect was arrested. At the jury trial, the lawyer for the accused admitted that his client did strike Officer Orrison but argued that other people did as well and that any of the folks involved in the brawl could have been the one who provided the lethal blow. The jury found the defendant as not guilty of the crimes of murder or manslaughter of Brunswick Officer William Orrison.

It is hypothesized that Officer William Orrison is still walking the beat in Downtown Brunswick, twirling his baton and still checking on doors of the local businesses located there. Is Officer Orrison still looking for the person who killed him? Does Officer Orrison even know he is deceased? One only wonders, but we do know one thing for sure...... Officer William Orrison of the Brunswick Police Department is eternally vigilant and continues to protect and serve Brunswick's residents.

POSTLUDE

The years pass us by so swiftly. We, too, swiftly pass from here to there. Do our footprints remain? Does our spirit remain? Where does our soul go? To Heaven? Is there a Hell? Why do some spirits remain, seeming to forever search for .... something or......someone. Perhaps one day, we will find out, and until this activity is deemed normal many of us investigate the paranormal.

Special Request

Have you or someone you know experienced paranormal activity in the greater Brunswick area? Have you seen a ghost? Have you seen a creature you couldn't identify? Do you have a myth or local legend to share?

If you answer yes to any of these questions, this author would love to hear from you. You can email him at jamesrcastle@comcast.net or type up your encounter and mail to:

James R. Castle
PO Box 8
Brunswick, MD 21716

ABOUT THE AUTHOR

James R. Castle was born and raised in the Brunswick, Maryland area. James delved into owning his own business upon graduating from Brunswick High School. Castle was elected twice to the Brunswick City Council in 2000 and 2005. He has volunteered for numerous Brunswick nonprofits including Brunswick Little League and the Brunswick Potomac Foundation; the owners and operators of the Brunswick Heritage Museum. James is a Brunswick, Maryland historian who has published numerous books about the history of the city. History in Our Attics, Photos and Documents of Brunswick, MD, Volume I was published in 2014 followed by Volume II in 2015. Volume III was published in 2018. The short story, A Christmas Trip to Brunswick was published in 2016.

Castle was named Tourism Ambassador for Frederick County in 2015 by Visit Frederick, Frederick County's tourism's association. In 2016, he received an award for historic preservation from the Frederick County Chapter of the Daughters of the American Revolution. In 2019, he was named as one of Frederick County's top 50 CEO's by the Frederick County Office of Economic Development for his work with the Brunswick Heritage Museum. James was awarded the Harrison Volunteer of the Year award in 2020 from Preservation Maryland.

OTHER BOOKS BY
JAMES R. CASTLE

History In Our Attics:

Photos and Document of Brunswick, Maryland

Volume I

Published 2014

www.jamesrcastle.com

History In Our Attics:

Photos and Document of Brunswick, Maryland

Volume II

Published 2015

www.jamesrcastle.com

A Christmas Trip To Brunswick

Published 2017

www.Jamesrcastle.com

History In Our Attics:

Photos and Documents of Brunswick, Maryland

Volume III

Published 2018

www.jamesrcastle.com

YouTube

James R. Castle

All books available on Amazon

RESOURCES

Alex Matsuo, www.alexmatsuo.com

Association of Paranormal Study,
www.associationofparanormalstudy.com

Brunswick Ghost and History Walks, Brunswick
Heritage Museum, www.brunswickmuseum.org

Brunswick Heritage Museum, 40 West Potomac
Street, Brunswick, MD 21716.
www.Brunswickmuseum.org

Brunswick History Commission,
www.brunswickhistory.com

Elite Paranormal Society,
www.eliteparanormalsociety.com

Frederick News Post Archives, www.fredericknewspost.newspaperarchive.com

Funk, H.B., Smith: Way Before We Were Brunswick, Self-Published

The Ghost Pit, www.facebook.com/paranormal219

Guidance and Insight With Sharon, Sharon Renner Lewis, www.facebook.com/pg/guidanceandinsightwithsharon

Maryland Society for Paranormal Research, www.msprparanormal.com

National Archives, U.S. National Archives and Records Administration

Peterson, Don, Native American Fish Traps in the Potomac River, Brunswick, MD", Self-Published, Revised 2020

Smoketown Brewing Station, 223 West Potomac Street, Brunswick, MD 21716, www.smoketownbrewing.com

Smoketown History Facebook Page, www.facebook.com/Smoketown-History-Brunswick-Md-307806060207